The Beast

by

Michaela Morgan

Illustrated by Chris Mould

Published in 2004 in Great Britain by
Barrington Stoke Ltd, Sandeman House, Trunk's Close,
55 High Street, Edinburgh EH1 1SR

ISBN 1-842991-98-1

Printed in Great Britain by Bell & Bain Ltd

Barrington Stoke gratefully acknowledges support from the
Scottish Arts Council towards the publication of the
gr8reads series

Scottish
Arts Council
LOTTERY FUNDED

A Note from the Author

The idea for *The Beast* came from a real story in a newspaper. Also, I used to live in the country where people told stories about a large beast like a big black cat. They said it looked a bit like a puma or a panther. They said it ate sheep – and pets. Is this the beast that the boys in my story hear howling in the woods? You'll have to read on to find out ...

Contents

Chapter 1
Star!

I was a star! It was cool! Very cool!

Men with cameras were all around us taking photos. There were women taking photos too.

One woman had a tape recorder.

Flash! went one camera.

Flash! went another.

"Look this way!" yelled one woman.

"Smile!" yelled another.

"You're both stars!" smiled the woman with the tape recorder. "Tell me all about it," she said.

The woman was from a newspaper. She told us her name was Jo.

"I want you to tell me all about what you did," she said. "We want to put you on TV on Saturday morning. Would you like that?"

"YEAH!" we both said.

"First things first," said Jo. "Would you like something to eat? A burger?"

We nodded. "Yeah! You bet!"

We all went to the big burger bar on West Street. We sat down at a table.

"What do you want?" she asked. "You can have anything you like. Anything at all."

This is what I had:

a burger, large fries, an extra large Coke, apple pie and ice cream with all the bits on.

Gaz had the same – but he asked for two burgers. He can be a bit of a pig.

Jo got all the stuff and put it down on the table. "Eat up!" she said.

She opened her bag and took out her notebook, a pen and a small tape recorder.

"There are some things I want to ask you," she said.

Chapter 2

Burgers, Chips and ... Questions

Jo looked at me. She opened her notebook. "What's your full name?" she asked.

"Robert Kevin Smith," I said, "but they all call me Robbie."

Then she looked at my mate. "And you," she said. "What's your name?"

"Gareth Jones – call me Gaz," Gaz told her.

His mouth was full of chips and he spat out little bits when he spoke. I told you he's a bit of a pig.

She wrote our names down in her notebook.

"And how old are you both?"

"14," we both spoke at the same time.
"But I'm going to be 15 soon," I said.

"OK," said Jo. She switched on her tape
recorder. "Now how did this all begin?"

She looked at Gaz. His mouth was still full of food. Then she looked at me and said, "Robbie, you start. Tell me your story ..."

Chapter 3
Robbie's Story

I had a sip of Coke and started my story.

"It all started one Monday night," I said.
"I was hanging around with Gaz. That's
what we do every night. We were in the
woods near my house. It was about 5 or
6 o'clock and just getting dark.

It gets dark early in November. There was a chill in the air. The shadows were getting longer and longer. The wind in the trees made a soft, sad sound.

We were thinking about going home before it got *really* dark, when it started. That sound ...

'OOOOOOooooOOOOOOOOooooooooooo,' it went.

'Listen,' said Gaz.

'*OooooOOOOooo.*'

It was a sort of ... howling. A spooky sort of howling. To me it sounded like a ghost. Gaz said it sounded like a wolf – or a werewolf. It was a *really* spooky sound."

"What did you do?" asked Jo.

"At first, we didn't do anything," I said. "We *couldn't* do anything. We just sat as still as stones.

We listened and looked at each other. I felt scared stiff. I was shivering. Then we heard the howling again and we didn't stop to think ..."

"What did you do then?" asked Jo.

"We ran," I said. "We ran and ran and ran. We ran like the wind and we didn't stop running until we were home.

At home I tried to forget about it. I watched TV as I always did. I went to bed as I always did. But that night I had bad dreams …"

"Me too," said Gaz, "I had really bad dreams – about werewolves and spooks."

Chapter 4

Is it a Werewolf?
Is it a Spook?

"The next day at school I talked to Gaz about it.

'It could be a beast,' I said.

'A what?' said Gaz.

'A beast! A wild animal!

I've heard that in some places there are
still beasts – like wild cats. Nobody knows
what they are, but lots of people say they
have seen big wild cats. They take photos
of them and sell them to the newspapers.'

Gaz looked up at me. 'The newspapers?' he said. 'Do they get paid for these photos? Do they get to be stars?'

'You bet,' I said.

We both wanted to be stars – to be rich and famous. 'Let's go for it,' I said.

So we made a plan to go to the woods again after school."

Chapter 5
The Woods

"After school we took a camera and set off for the woods. We wanted to get there before it got dark.

We crept around the woods, not making a sound. We crept around and we stopped to look and listen. We spoke very softly.

All the time I was waiting for a ghost or a wolf or a beast to jump out of the trees. And do you know what? There was nothing there. We didn't hear a thing. We didn't see a thing. We felt a bit silly.

'It must have been an owl,' said Gaz. 'We were scared of an owl!'

'We'll just forget all about it,' Gaz said.

'OK,' I said. 'We'll forget all about it.'

We both felt stupid!"

Chapter 6
Saturday

"The next time we went to the woods it was Saturday – 3 days later. We were just hanging around, having a laugh. Gaz was having a go at me and I was having a go at him.

'Do you remember the night we heard that howling?' he said. 'You went as white as a ghost.'

'So did you!' I said. 'You were shaking like a jelly. And then you ran! I have NEVER seen you run as fast as that in your life. Never! I didn't know you *could* run like that! Next sports day I know what to do to get you to run. I'll go "OOOOooOOOoooo," and you'll be off like a shot.'

'*OooooOOOoo*,' Gaz went, and we flapped about like ghosts, howling and swooping and laughing at each other.

Then we heard it. A howling.

'Was that you, Gaz?' I asked.

'No, was it you?'

The howling sound came again. It was a long, sad sound. We looked at each other. 'It wasn't me. It wasn't you,' I said. 'S ... so what was it?'

'*OooOOOOooo.*'

The howling started again.

'*OooooooOOOOOooo.*'

And once again we ran."

Chapter 7
The Fight

"We'd made up our minds that there was something spooky in the woods.

It could be a beast. Or a wolf. Or a ghost.

At school we told some other boys about it. And do you know what they did? They laughed at us. They laughed their heads off! They laughed and laughed and laughed. I've always hated being laughed at. I felt myself going red.

'Cut it out!' I yelled, but they went on laughing and laughing and laughing – and that's how the fight started.

In the end I had to stay late after school. So did Gaz. He had tried to help me in the fight. It was nearly dark as we were walking home from school.

'That's it!' said Gaz. 'We don't say another word about spooky sounds in the woods. We don't even think about spooky sounds in the woods.'

'OK! Let's go home another way,' I said. I didn't want to walk anywhere near the woods.

That night, safe in my bed, I was just starting to fall asleep when I heard it again. The far-away sound of howling was coming from the woods at the back of my house.

It sounded very, very far-away.

'Oooooooo*OOO*ooo*OOO*ooooo.'

It's a dream, I told myself – but I sat up and listened again.

'Oooooooo*OOO*ooo*OOO*ooooo.'

Maybe it's the wind, I said to myself.
Maybe it's a bird. Maybe it's an owl.

I tried to go to sleep.

The next day at school I went to find
Gaz.

'I heard that sound again,' I said,
'I heard it last night. We have to go back
one last time. I can't just forget about it.'

'Oh no,' Gaz moaned. 'Just drop it!'

He didn't want to go. But he's a good friend, so that night after school he went back with me. This time we took a camera and a torch, and we took a mobile phone.

'If we find something, we can phone for help,' I said. 'Look. I've dialled 999 but I haven't pressed CALL. As soon as we find the beast we press CALL. Then we run. OK?'

'OK,' Gaz said, but he didn't look very keen.

Into the woods we went. I looked at Gaz. His face was pale and he was shivering.

'What if there *is* a beast?' he said. 'What if it comes after us?'

'I've told you. We just press CALL on the phone and the police will be here to save us.'

'Or the ambulance men will be here to pick up our half-eaten bodies,' Gaz moaned.

We looked for the place where we'd been when we'd heard the noise before. Gaz was keen on having a quick look around and then getting back home.

'I think it was over here somewhere,' said Gaz.

'No, I think it was over there,' I said, 'by that tree.'

We stood there.

We kept very still.

We listened.

We heard nothing.

'Right,' said Gaz. 'We've been back.
We've looked around. We've listened. Now
let's go home.'

Then we heard something.

It wasn't a howling sound.

It was panting. Something was panting
loudly very near to us."

Chapter 8
The Beast

"I looked all around but all I could see were trees and shadows. It was very still. The trees seemed to be getting closer to us. The shadows were getting longer.

Then ...

'*OOooOOOOOoo*,'

... the sound.

It was very close now, but very soft, like the wind in the trees.

'Let's get out of here.' Gaz turned to run. I grabbed him.

'It's coming from behind that tree,' I said softly. 'Listen!'

We stood still and we listened.

The sound of my own heart scared me.

It was thumping. 'Boom, boom, boom,' it

went. Then we heard a scratching,

'Scritch.'

'Scratch.'

'S-C-R-A-T-C-H.'

Then there was silence.

I pulled the long grass to one side. My heart was still thumping.

'What is it?' Gaz asked.

'I think it's an old drain,' I said. 'It's some sort of old pipe.'

We listened.

'There's nothing there,' said Gaz, and then, 'Oh, what's THAT?'

We could hear the panting again – and a scratching noise. Something was trying to scratch its way towards us."

Chapter 9
Glowing Eyes

"Gaz grabbed the phone and the torch and was going to run – but I stopped him.

'Wait!' I said.

'Keep your hand on the phone,' I said to him. 'I'm going to have a look.'

I looked into the dark hole.

It was black as black. I couldn't see a thing.

Then ...

'Aaaaaaaaaaaaaaaa!'

I gave a yell. I was about to run.

'What did you see? What did you see?' Gaz asked.

I couldn't breathe. 'I saw eyes!' I said.
'Eyes glowing in the dark! There's
something in there!'

'OOOoooOOOooo.'

The sound came again and Gaz pressed CALL on the phone."

Chapter 10

In Trouble with the Police?

"Some time later the police came. It was one policeman and one policewoman.

A gang of kids came too. They had heard the police car and they'd come to see what was going on. I could see some boys from my class. They were all ready to laugh at me and Gaz.

'What's this all about?' said the policeman. 'What did you say you'd heard?'

'Is this some sort of joke?' asked the policewoman.

'No!' said Gaz. 'It's true. There's some sort of beast here – a wolf, or a ...'

Behind him the boys were laughing. The police were just about to march us home and tell our parents.

'OOooOOOOoo.'

They heard it too. They looked at each other and they looked at us.

'I think these boys may have been telling the truth,' said the policewoman.

'Let's take a look!'

They went to have a look.

'Hello!' the policeman shouted down the drain.

'Helloooo,' a spooky voice replied.

Gaz looked at me. His face was white.

'Is there anybody there?' yelled the policeman.

'Anybody there ...' said the spooky voice.

'It's just an echo,' said the policewoman.

'There *is* something there!' I said. 'There *is*! Can't you see 2 glowing eyes?'

'No,' said the policeman. 'I can't see 2 eyes ...'

Then he looked round at me.

'I can see 4!' he said."

Chapter 11
Trapped!

"The boys behind us stopped laughing.

The policeman stopped smiling. 'I'll send for back-up,' he said.

Soon two more police cars and a van with a team of men came.

They pulled away the twigs and long grass and started to dig.

We stood well back and watched. Every now and then the men took a rest and we would all stop and listen. First it was a scratching. Then a howling. And then a *woof*!

'It's a dog!' said Gaz.

But it wasn't a dog. It was two dogs. They had been trapped there for weeks. You should have seen them. They were so thin – just skin and bone. They were so thin you could see all of their ribs."

Chapter 12
Watch this Space!

Jo, the reporter, shut her notebook.
"I know the rest," she said. "The dogs'
owners were very glad to get them back.
You'll get a big reward."

"And none of those boys at school are
laughing at us now!" I said.

Jo switched off her tape recorder. "Well, now I know the whole story," she said, "I'll write it up. If you watch TV on Saturday, you'll see your story. I think it will be in the newspapers too. Look out for it. You're going to be stars."

Well, we did look out for it and it *was* in the newspapers.

There was a big photo of me and Gaz in the local paper. We were even in the *Mail* and the *Sun*. It's true. Here is just one of the cuttings:

I've cut out all the newspaper stories
and stuck them on my bedroom wall.
On Saturday, Gaz and all my mates from
school are coming to my house to watch TV.

We're all going to watch the story they
made about us for the TV. It's called *The*

Beast and it stars two boys who are playing the parts of me and Gaz. We're going to be big stars. I can't wait!

Barrington Stoke would like to thank all its readers for commenting on the manuscript before publication and in particular:

Katie Burnell

Zoe Davies

Clare Deakin

Adam Fowler

Mrs Doreen Gilmour

Shaunna McCubbin

Sylvia Petty

Sarah Poole

Glen Shannon

Become a Consultant!

Would you like to give us feedback on our titles before they are published? Contact us at the address below – we'd love to hear from you!

Barrington Stoke, Sandeman House, Trunk's Close, 55 High Street, Edinburgh EH1 1SR
Tel: 0131 557 2020 Fax: 0131 557 6060
E-mail: info@barringtonstoke.co.uk
Website: www.barringtonstoke.co.uk

If you loved this book, why don't you read ...

Torrent!

by

Bernard Ashley
ISBN 1-842991-96-5

RUN 4 YOUR LIFE!

Tod thinks he's going to die. The dam's broken. He's trapped.
He must get to the bridge before it's swept away! Who can save him now?